Grandma's List

Sometimes my Grandma forgets.

I want her to remember the important things,
so I help her make lists.

Grandkids		
grandkid · age · birthday		
Joey	12	Aug. 5
Nicky	10	Apr. 6
Kristy	9	Sept. 30
Maria	7	Mar. 17

We made a list of her grandkids.

We made a list of her friends and their phone numbers.

We made a list of her favorite things.

We made a list of things we like to do together.

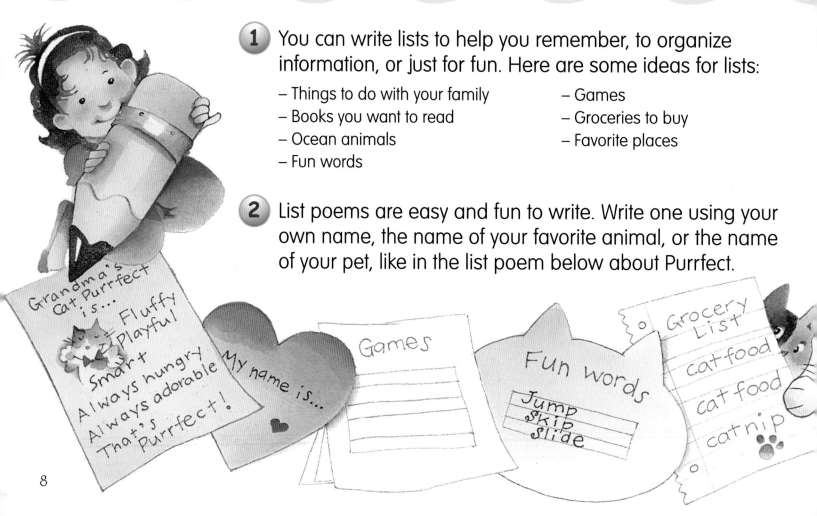

1. You can write lists to help you remember, to organize information, or just for fun. Here are some ideas for lists:

   – Things to do with your family
   – Books you want to read
   – Ocean animals
   – Fun words

   – Games
   – Groceries to buy
   – Favorite places

2. List poems are easy and fun to write. Write one using your own name, the name of your favorite animal, or the name of your pet, like in the list poem below about Purrfect.

Grandma's Cat Purrfect is...
Fluffy
Playful
Smart
Always hungry
Always adorable
That's Purrfect!

My name is...

Games

Fun words
Jump
Skip
Slide

Grocery List
cat food
cat food
catnip

8